Hanukkah Hamster

By **Michelle Markel** and Illustrated by **André Ceolin**

PUBLISHED by SLEEPING BEAR PRESS

To Lana, with love
—Michelle

For my wife, Gracy, and my son, Gabriel, who always stood by me.
For Mela, who has been doing a lot for my career.
—André

December had come to the city.
Decorations glittered on rooftops and windows.

People rushed in and out of stores
to buy gifts for the holidays.

All day long Edgar drove them in his cab.

At the end of his shift, he was so tired! He climbed into the backseat of his cab and took a little nap.

Ohhhf! Something scrambled onto his chest.

Ayyee! Something hairy brushed his face.

Was it a dream?

No! It was a hamster.

Edgar scooped it up.

The hamster settled into his hand.
Its feet were so pink and teeny!
Two beady black eyes blinked.

Edgar stroked the hamster's back and then
set it in his lunch bag.

He wondered who'd left the hamster in the cab.
But so many customers had gotten in and out!
Edgar phoned in a report to Lost and Found at the cab company.

At his apartment, using a cardboard box and shredded paper,
Edgar made a home for the hamster.

"There you go."

He said the Hanukkah blessings. And while the night stars watched, he lit two candles on the menorah.

The next day, Edgar drove more people on their holiday errands.

He got a message from Lost and Found saying that nobody had called about the hamster.

That night, after lighting three candles, Edgar made chopped salad—the kind he used to eat back home— and he minced a tiny one for the hamster.

"You and me again."

Edgar looked at the cucumbers and chickpeas on his plate. Then he watched the hamster nibble on its own salad.

"Okay if I call you Chickpea?"

The following night, Edgar stopped at the lost and found desk.
"Has anybody called about the hamster?"

The manager shook her head.

Edgar looked at hamster supplies at a pet shop.
He counted the tip money in his pockets—enough for a nice wheel.
I really shouldn't, Edgar thought, so instead he just bought food.

When he got home, he said the blessings and lit four candles.

Chickpea got into the bowl with his hamster food.

He did a backflip.

Was that a little smile?

Edgar took pictures on his phone and shared them with his family in Israel.

Day five of Hanukkah dawned cold and brisk.

Throughout his shift, Edgar stopped his cab to check for messages, but no one had claimed the hamster.

That night he made a slide out of a cardboard tube.
Chickpea whooshed down. *Wheeee!* His nose twitched.

On days six and seven of Hanukkah, Edgar had a sinking feeling.
Someone might be missing the little hamster.
Someone might be about to call.

While the Hanukkah candles burned down, Edgar told Chickpea about Tel Aviv—about the outdoor cafés, the palm trees, the warm breezes. He petted him on his black stripe and the hamster fell asleep.

The next morning, Edgar drove a customer to the outskirts of town. When he stopped the cab, the houses looked familiar. So did a woman standing in front of one of them, with a boy.

She was a woman he'd driven a few days ago.
And that must be her son.

Edgar felt a punch in his heart.

He made himself wave and roll down the window.

"Little boy," he called, "did you lose your hamster?"

"The hamster!" the boy cried.

"I bought him for my classroom," the woman said.
"He disappeared the same day."

She looked closely at Edgar.
"But I didn't think he escaped during the cab ride."

"We thought he was hiding in the bedding," the boy said.
"Then we saw that the cage door was loose."

Edgar showed them pictures on his phone.
"I've been calling him Chickpea.
Here he is eating salad—his favorite.
Here he is going down the slide.

look at his black stripe—he loves it when you pet him there."

The woman squinted down at one of the photos.
"Do I see a menorah?"

"Yes," said Edgar. "Me and the hamster,
we've been celebrating Hanukkah together."

"You and the hamster," the woman said. "Do you have family here?"

"No, they're back in Israel."

"So you live by yourself?"

Edgar nodded.

"Oh. It was very kind of you to take care
of the hamster, and to let us know."

"No trouble at all," Edgar said. "You picked out a good one."

He took a deep breath. "So, I have to return him to you.
Tomorrow, before work, I . . . I can . . ."

The boy touched his mother's arm,
and the two of them exchanged glances.

"I think this hamster belongs with *you*,"
the woman said to Edgar. "He looks right at home!"

She reached out to shake his hand
and wished him a wonderful holiday.

That evening, while the stars shone above the kitchen window,
Edgar said the blessings and lit all the candles on the menorah.
He set out a doughnut for himself and a new wheel for his friend.

"Happy Hanukkah, Chickpea!"